THIS
BOOK BELONGS
TO

Little Wizard Stories of Oz

by L. Frank Baum
Illustrated by John R. Neill

BOOKS OF WONDER
WILLIAM MORROW AND COMPANY
New York

To create this new edition of L. Frank Baum's *Little Wizard Stories of Oz,* we obtained twenty-eight different first editions, which were generously loaned to us from private collections. We wish to thank the following, who were so generous with their treasures: William Campbell, Bruce and Gail Crockett, Dr. Carol Faget, Barbara Koelle, Patrick M. Maund, David Maxine, Mrs. Carl Shirley, and Bonnie Vitti.

Little Wizard Stories of Oz

Contents

The Cowardly Lion and the Hungry Tiger   15

Little Dorothy and Toto   39

Tiktok and the Nome King   63

Ozma and the Little Wizard   87

Jack Pumpkinhead and the Sawhorse   111

The Scarecrow and the Tin Woodman   135

THE COWARDLY LION AND
THE HUNGRY TIGER

I N the splendid palace of the Emerald City, which is in the center of the fairy Land of Oz, is a great Throne Room, where Princess Ozma, the Ruler, for an hour each day sits in a throne of glistening emeralds and listens to all the troubles of her people, which they are sure to tell her about. Around Ozma's throne, on such occasions, are grouped all

the important personages of Oz, such as the Scarecrow, Jack Pumpkinhead, Tiktok the Clockwork Man, the Tin Woodman, the Wizard of Oz, the Shaggy Man and other famous fairy people. Little Dorothy usually has a seat at Ozma's feet, and crouched on either side the throne are two enormous beasts known as the Hungry Tiger and the Cowardly Lion.

These two beasts are Ozma's chief guardians, but as everyone loves the beautiful girl Princess there has never been any disturbance in the great Throne Room, or anything for the guardians to do but look fierce and solemn and keep quiet until the Royal Audience is over and the people go away to their homes.

Of course no one would dare be naughty while the huge Lion and Tiger crouched beside the throne; but the fact is, the people of Oz are very seldom naughty. So Ozma's big guards are more ornamental than useful, and no one realizes that better than the beasts themselves.

One day, after everybody had left the Throne Room except the Cowardly Lion and the Hungry Tiger, the Lion yawned and said to his friend:

"I'm getting tired of this job. No one is afraid of us and no one pays any attention to us."

"That is true," replied the big Tiger, purring softly. "We might as well be in the thick jungles where we were born, as trying to protect Ozma when she needs no protection. And I'm dreadfully hungry all the time."

"You have enough to eat, I'm sure," said the Lion, swaying his tail slowly back and forth.

"Enough, perhaps; but not the kind of food I long for," answered the Tiger. "What I'm hungry for is fat babies. I have a great desire to eat a few fat babies. Then, perhaps, the people of Oz would fear me and I'd become more important."

"True," agreed the Lion. "It would stir up quite a rumpus if you ate but *one* fat baby. As for myself, my claws are sharp as needles and strong as crowbars, while my teeth are powerful enough to tear a person to

pieces in a few seconds. If I should spring upon a man and make chop suey of him, there would be wild excitement in the Emerald City and the people would fall upon their knees and beg me for mercy. That, in my opinion, would render me of considerable importance."

"After you had torn the person to pieces, what would you do next?" asked the Tiger sleepily.

"Then I would roar so loudly it would shake the earth and stalk away to the jungle to hide myself, before anyone could attack me or kill me for what I had done."

"I see," nodded the Tiger. "You are really cowardly."

"To be sure. That is why I am named the

Cowardly Lion. That is why I have always been so tame and peaceable. But I'm awfully tired of being tame," added the Lion, with a sigh, "and it would be fun to raise a row and show people what a terrible beast I really am."

The Tiger remained silent for several minutes, thinking deeply as he slowly washed his face with his left paw. Then he said:

"I'm getting old, and it would please me to eat at least one fat baby before I die. Suppose we surprise these people of Oz and prove our power. What do you say? We will walk out of here just as usual and the first baby we meet I'll eat in a jiffy, and the first man or woman you meet you will tear to pieces. Then we will both run out of the city gates and gallop across the country and hide in the jungle before anyone can stop us."

"All right; I'm game," said the Lion, yawning again so that he showed two rows of dreadfully sharp teeth.

The Tiger got up and stretched his great, sleek body.

"Come on," he said. The Lion stood up and proved he was the larger of the two, for he was almost as big as a small horse.

Out of the palace they walked, and met no one. They passed through the beautiful grounds, past fountains and beds of lovely flowers, and met no one. Then they un-latched a gate and entered a street of the city, and met no one.

"I wonder how a fat baby will taste," remarked the Tiger, as they stalked majestically along, side by side.

"I imagine it will taste like nutmegs," said the Lion.

"No," said the Tiger, "I've an idea it will taste like gumdrops."

They turned a corner, but met no one, for the people of the Emerald City were accustomed to take their naps at this hour of the afternoon.

"I wonder how many pieces I ought to tear a person into," said the Lion, in a thoughtful voice.

"Sixty would be about right," suggested the Tiger.

"Would that hurt any more than to tear

one into about a dozen pieces?" inquired the Lion, with a little shudder.

"Who cares whether it hurts or not?" growled the Tiger.

The Lion did not reply. They entered a side street, but met no one.

Suddenly they heard a child crying.

"Aha!" exclaimed the Tiger. "There is my meat."

He rushed around a corner, the Lion following, and came upon a nice fat baby sitting in the middle of the street and crying as if in great distress.

"What's the matter?" asked the Tiger, crouching before the baby.

"I—I—l-lost my m-m-mamma!" wailed the baby.

"Why, you poor little thing," said the great beast, softly stroking the child's head with its paw. "Don't cry, my dear, for mamma can't be far away and I'll help you to find her."

"Go on," said the Lion, who stood by.

"Go on where?" asked the Tiger, looking up.

"Go on and eat your fat baby."

"Why, you dreadful creature!" said the Tiger reproachfully; "would you want me to eat a poor little lost baby, that doesn't know where its mother is?" And the beast gathered the little one into its strong, hairy arms and tried to comfort it by rocking it gently back and forth.

The Lion growled low in his throat and

seemed very much disappointed; but at
that moment a scream reached their ears
and a woman came bounding out of a house
and into the street. Seeing her baby in the
embrace of the monster Tiger the woman
screamed again and rushed forward to rescue it, but in her haste she caught her foot
in her skirt and tumbled head over heels
and heels over head, stopping with such a
bump that she saw many stars in the heav-
ens, although it was broad daylight. And
there she lay, in a helpless manner, all tangled up and unable to stir.

With one bound and a roar like thunder
the huge Lion was beside her. With his
strong jaws he grasped her dress and
raised her into an upright position.

"Poor thing! Are you hurt?" he gently asked.

Gasping for breath the woman struggled to free herself and tried to walk, but she limped badly and tumbled down again.

"My baby!" she said pleadingly.

"The baby is all right; don't worry," replied the Lion; and then he added: "Keep quiet, now, and I'll carry you back to your house, and the Hungry Tiger will carry your baby."

The Tiger, who had approached the place with the child in its arms, asked in astonishment:

"Aren't you going to tear her into sixty pieces?"

"No, nor into six pieces," answered the

Lion indignantly. "I'm not such a brute as to destroy a poor woman who has hurt herself trying to save her lost baby. If you are so ferocious and cruel and bloodthirsty, you may leave me and go away, for I do not care to associate with you."

"That's all right," answered the Tiger. "I'm not cruel—not in the least—I'm only hungry. But I thought *you* were cruel."

"Thank heaven I'm respectable," said the Lion, with dignity. He then raised the woman and with much gentleness carried her into her house, where he laid her upon a sofa. The Tiger followed with the baby, which he safely deposited beside its mother. The little one liked the Hungry Tiger and grasping the enormous beast by both ears the baby kissed the beast's nose to show he was grateful and happy.

"Thank you very much," said the woman. "I've often heard what good beasts you are, in spite of your power to do mischief to mankind, and now I know that the stories are true. I do not think either of you have ever had an evil thought."

The Hungry Tiger and the Cowardly Lion hung their heads and did not look into each other's eyes, for both were shamed and humbled. They crept away and stalked back through the streets until they again entered the palace grounds, where they retreated to the pretty, comfortable rooms they occupied at the back of the palace. There they silently crouched in their

usual corners to think over their adventure.

After a while the Tiger said sleepily:

"I don't believe fat babies taste like gumdrops. I'm quite sure they have the flavor of raspberry tarts. My, how hungry I am for fat babies!"

The Lion grunted disdainfully.

"You're a humbug," said he.

"Am I?" retorted the Tiger, with a sneer. "Tell me, then, into how many pieces you usually tear your victims, my bold Lion?"

The Lion impatiently thumped the floor with his tail.

"To tear anyone into pieces would soil my claws and blunt my teeth," he said. "I'm glad I didn't muss myself up this afternoon by hurting that poor mother."

The Tiger looked at him steadily and then yawned a wide, wide yawn.

"You're a coward," he remarked.

"Well," said the Lion, "it's better to be a coward than to do wrong."

"To be sure," answered the other. "And that reminds me that I nearly lost my own reputation. For, had I eaten that fat baby, I would not now be the Hungry Tiger. It's better to go hungry, seems to me, than to be cruel to a little child."

And then they dropped their heads on their paws and went to sleep.

LITTLE DOROTHY AND TOTO

 OROTHY was a little Kansas girl who once accidentally found the beautiful Land of Oz and was invited to live there always. Toto was Dorothy's small black dog, with fuzzy, curly hair and bright black eyes. Together, when they tired of the grandeur of the Emerald City of Oz, they would wander out into the country and all through the land,

peering into queer nooks and corners and having a good time in their own simple way. There was a little Wizard living in Oz who was a faithful friend of Dorothy and did not approve of her traveling alone in this way, but the girl always laughed at the little man's fears for her and said she was not afraid of anything that might happen.

One day, while on such a journey, Dorothy and Toto found themselves among the wild wooded hills at the southeast of Oz—a place usually avoided by travelers because so many magical things abounded there. And, as they entered a forest path, the little girl noticed a sign tacked to a tree, which said: "Look out for Crinklink."

Toto could not talk, as many of the animals of Oz can, for he was just a common Kansas dog; but he looked at the sign so seriously that Dorothy almost believed he could read it, and she knew quite well that Toto understood every word she said to him.

"Never mind Crinklink," said she. "I don't believe anything in Oz will try to hurt us, Toto, and if I get into trouble you must take care of me."

"Bow-wow!" said Toto, and Dorothy knew that meant a promise.

The path was narrow and wound here and there between the trees, but they could not lose their way, because thick vines and creepers shut them in on both sides. They had walked a long time when, suddenly

turning a curve of the pathway, they came upon a lake of black water, so big and so deep that they were forced to stop.

"Well, Toto," said Dorothy, looking at the lake, "we must turn back, I guess, for there is neither a bridge nor a boat to take us across the black water."

"Here's the ferryman, though," cried a tiny voice beside them, and the girl gave a start and looked down at her feet, where a man no taller than three inches sat at the edge of the path with his legs dangling over the lake.

"Oh!" said Dorothy; "I didn't see you before."

Toto growled fiercely and made his ears stand up straight, but the little man did not seem in the least afraid of the dog. He merely repeated: "I'm the ferryman, and it's my business to carry people across the lake."

Dorothy couldn't help feeling surprised, for she could have picked the little man up with one hand, and the lake was big and broad. Looking at the ferryman more closely she saw that he had small eyes, a big nose, and a sharp chin. His hair was blue and his clothes scarlet, and Dorothy noticed that every button on his jacket was the head of some animal. The top button was a bear's head and the next button a wolf's head; the next was a cat's head and the next a weasel's head, while the last button of all was the head of a field-mouse. When

Dorothy looked into the eyes of these animals' heads, they all nodded and said in a chorus: "Don't believe all you hear, little girl!"

"Silence!" said the small ferryman, slapping each button head in turn, but not hard enough to hurt them. Then he turned to Dorothy and asked: "Do you wish to cross over the lake?"

"Why, I'd like to," she answered, hesitating; "but I can't see how you will manage to carry us, without any boat."

"If you can't see, you mustn't see," he answered with a laugh. "All you need do is shut your eyes, say the word, and—over you go!"

Dorothy wanted to get across, in order

that she might continue her journey.

"All right," she said, closing her eyes; "I'm ready."

Instantly she was seized in a pair of strong arms—arms so big and powerful that she was startled and cried out in fear.

"Silence!" roared a great voice, and the girl opened her eyes to find that the tiny man had suddenly grown to a giant and was holding both her and Toto in a tight embrace while in one step he spanned the lake and reached the other shore.

Dorothy became frightened, then, especially as the giant did not stop but continued tramping in great steps over the wooded hills, crushing bushes and trees beneath his broad feet. She struggled in vain to free herself, while Toto whined and trembled beside her, for the little dog was frightened, too.

"Stop!" screamed the girl. "Let me down!" But the giant paid no attention. "Who are you, and where are you taking me?" she continued; but the giant said not a word. Close to Dorothy's ear, however, a voice answered her, saying: "This is the terrible Crinklink, and he has you in his power."

Dorothy managed to twist her head around and found it was the second button on the jacket—the wolf's head—which had spoken to her.

"What will Crinklink do with me?" she asked anxiously.

"No one knows. You must wait and see," replied the wolf.

"Some of his captives he whips," squeaked the weasel's head.

"Some he transforms into bugs and other things," growled the bear's head.

"Some he enchants, so that they become doorknobs," sighed the cat's head.

"Some he makes his slaves—even as we are—and that is the most dreadful fate of all," added the field-mouse. "As long as Crinklink exists we shall remain buttons, but as there are no more buttonholes on his jacket he will probably make you a slave."

Dorothy began to wish she had not met Crinklink. Meantime, the giant took such big steps that he soon reached the heart

of the hills, where, perched upon the highest peak, stood a log castle. Before this castle he paused to set down Dorothy and Toto, for Crinklink was at present far too large to enter his own doorway. So he made himself grow smaller, until he was about the size of an ordinary man. Then he said to Dorothy, in stern, commanding tones:

"Enter, girl!"

Dorothy obeyed and entered the castle, with Toto at her heels. She found the place to be merely one big room. There was a table and chair of ordinary size near the center, and at one side a wee bed that seemed scarcely big enough for a doll. Everywhere else were dishes—dishes—dishes! They were all soiled, and were piled upon the floor, in all the corners and upon every shelf. Evidently Crinklink had not washed a dish for years, but had cast them aside as he used them.

Dorothy's captor sat down in the chair and frowned at her.

"You are young and strong, and will make a good dishwasher," said he.

"Do you mean me to wash all those dishes?" she asked, feeling both indignant and fearful, for such a task would take weeks to accomplish.

"That's just what I mean," he retorted. "I need clean dishes, for all I have are soiled, and you're going to make 'em clean or get trounced. So get to work and be careful not to break anything. If you smash a dish, the penalty is one lash from my dreadful cat-o'-nine-tails for every piece the dish breaks into," and here Crinklink displayed a terrible whip that made the little girl shudder.

Dorothy knew how to wash dishes, but she remembered that often she carelessly broke one. In this case, however, a good deal depended on being careful, so she handled the dishes very cautiously.

While she worked, Toto sat by the hearth and growled low at Crinklink, and Crinklink sat in his chair and growled at Dorothy because she moved so slowly. He expected her to break a dish any minute, but as the hours passed away and this did not happen Crinklink began to grow sleepy.

It was tiresome watching the girl wash
dishes and often he glanced longingly at the
tiny bed. Now he began to yawn, and he
yawned and yawned until finally he said:

"I'm going to take a nap. But the buttons
on my jacket will be wide awake and whenever you break a dish the crash will waken
me. As I'm rather sleepy I hope you won't
interrupt my nap by breaking anything for
a long time."

Then Crinklink made himself grow smaller and smaller until he was three inches
high and of a size to fit the tiny bed. At once
he lay down and fell fast asleep.

Dorothy came close to the buttons and
whispered: "Would you really warn Crinklink if I tried to escape?"

"You can't escape," growled the bear. "Crinklink would become a giant, and soon overtake you."

"But you might kill him while he sleeps," suggested the cat, in a soft voice.

"Oh!" cried Dorothy, drawing back; "I couldn't poss'bly *kill* anything—even to save my life."

But Toto had heard this conversation and was not so particular about killing monsters. Also the little dog knew he must try to save his mistress. In an instant he sprang upon the wee bed and was about to seize the sleeping Crinklink in his jaws when Dorothy heard a loud crash and a heap of dishes fell from the table to the floor. Then the girl saw Toto and the little man rolling on the floor together, like a fuzzy ball, and when the ball stopped rolling, behold! there was Toto wagging his tail joyfully and there sat the little Wizard of Oz, laughing merrily at the expression of surprise on Dorothy's face.

"Yes, my dear, it's me," said he, "and I've been playing tricks on you—for your own good. I wanted to prove to you that it is really dangerous for a little girl to wander alone in a fairy country; so I took the form of Crinklink to teach you a lesson. There isn't any Crinklink, to be sure; but if there had been you'd be severely whipped for breaking all those dishes."

The Wizard now rose, took off the coat with the button heads, and spread it on the

floor, wrong side up. At once there crept from beneath it a bear, a wolf, a cat, a weasel, and a field-mouse, who all rushed from the room and escaped into the mountains.

"Come on, Toto," said Dorothy; "let's go back to the Emerald City. You've given me a good scare, Wizard," she added, with dignity, "and p'raps I'll forgive you, by'n'by; but just now I'm mad to think how easily you fooled me."

TIKTOK AND
THE NOME KING

HE Nome King was unpleasantly angry. He had carelessly bitten his tongue at breakfast and it still hurt; so he roared and raved and stamped around in his underground palace in a way that rendered him very disagreeable.

It so happened that on this unfortunate day Tiktok, the Clockwork Man, visited the

Nome King to ask a favor. Tiktok lived in the Land of Oz, and although he was an active and important person, he was made entirely of metal. Machinery within him, something like the works of a clock, made him move; other machinery made him talk; still other machinery made him think.

Although so cleverly constructed, the Clockwork Man was far from perfect. Three separate keys wound up his motion machinery, his speech works, and his thoughts. One or more of these contrivances was likely to run down at a critical moment, leaving poor Tiktok helpless. Also some of his parts were wearing out, through much use, and just now his thought machinery needed repair. The skillful little Wizard of Oz had tinkered with Tiktok's thoughts without being able to get them properly regulated, so he had advised the Clockwork Man to go to the Nome King and secure a new set of springs, which would render his thoughts more elastic and responsive.

"Be careful what you say to the Nome King," warned the Wizard. "He has a bad temper and the least little thing makes him angry."

Tiktok promised, and the Wizard wound his machinery and set him walking in the direction of the Nome King's dominions, just across the desert from the Land of Oz. He ran down just as he reached the entrance to the underground palace, and there Kaliko, the Nome King's Chief Steward, found him and wound him up again.

"I want to see the King," said Tiktok, in his jerky voice.

"Well," remarked Kaliko, "it may be safe for a cast-iron person like you to face his Majesty this morning; but you must announce yourself, for should I show my face inside the jewel-studded cavern where the King is now raving, I'd soon look like a dish of mashed potatoes, and be of no further use to anyone."

"I'm not a-fraid," said Tiktok.

"Then walk in and make yourself at home," answered Kaliko, and threw open the door of the King's cavern.

Tiktok promptly walked in and faced the

astonished Nome King, to whom he said: "Good morn-ing. I want two new steel springs for my thought-works and a new cog-wheel for my speech-pro-du-cer. How a-bout it, your Maj-es-ty?"

The Nome King growled a menacing growl and his eyes were red with rage.

"How dare you enter my presence?" he shouted.

"I dare an-y-thing," said Tiktok. "I'm not a-fraid of a fat Nome."

This was true, yet an unwise speech. Had Tiktok's thoughts been in good working order he would have said something else. The angry Nome King quickly caught up his heavy mace and hurled it straight at Tiktok. When it struck the metal man's

breast, the force of the blow burst the bolts which held the plates of his body together and they clattered to the floor in a score of pieces. Hundreds and hundreds of wheels, pins, cogs and springs filled the air like a cloud and then rattled like hail upon the floor.

Where Tiktok had stood was now only a scrap-heap and the Nome King was so amazed by the terrible effect of his blow that he stared in wonder.

His Majesty's anger quickly cooled. He remembered that the Clockwork Man was a favorite subject of the powerful Princess, Ozma of Oz, who would be sure to resent Tiktok's ruin.

"Too bad! too bad!" he muttered, regretfully. "I'm really sorry I made junk of the fellow. I didn't know he'd break."

"You'd better be," remarked Kaliko, who now ventured to enter the room. "You'll have a war on your hands when Ozma hears of this, and the chances are you will lose your throne and your kingdom."

The Nome King turned pale, for he loved to rule the Nomes and did not know of any other way to earn a living in case Ozma fought and conquered him.

"Do—do you think Ozma will be angry?" he asked anxiously.

"I'm sure of it," said Kaliko. "And she has the right to be. You've made scrap-iron of her favorite."

The King groaned.

"Sweep him up and throw the rubbish into the black pit," he commanded; and then he shut himself up in his private den and for days would see no one, because he was so ashamed of his unreasoning anger and so feared the results of his rash act.

Kaliko swept up the pieces, but he did not throw them into the black pit. Being a clever and skillful mechanic he determined to fit the pieces together again.

No man ever faced a greater puzzle; but it was interesting work and Kaliko succeeded. When he found a spring or wheel worn or imperfect, he made a new one.

Within two weeks, by working steadily night and day, the Chief Steward completed his task and put the three sets of clock-

works and the last rivet into Tiktok's body. He then wound up the motion machinery, and the Clockwork Man walked up and down the room as naturally as ever. Then Kaliko wound up the thought works and the speech regulator and said to Tiktok:

"How do you feel now?"

"Fine," said the Clockwork Man. "You have done a ve-ry good job, Kal-i-ko, and saved me from de-struc-tion. Much o-bliged."

"Don't mention it," replied the Chief Steward. "I quite enjoyed the work."

Just then the Nome King's gong sound-ed, and Kaliko rushed away through the jewel-studded cavern and into the den where the King had hidden, leaving the doors ajar.

"Kaliko," said the King, in a meek voice, "I've been shut up here long enough to repent bitterly the destruction of Tiktok. Of course Ozma will have revenge, and send an army to fight us, but we must take our medicine. One thing comforts me: Tiktok wasn't really a live person; he was only a machine man, and so it wasn't very wicked to stop his clockworks. I couldn't sleep nights, at first, for worry; but there's no more harm in smashing a machine man than in breaking a wax doll. Don't you think so?"

"I am too humble to think in the presence of your Majesty," said Kaliko.

"Then get me something to eat," commanded the King, "for I'm nearly starved.

Two roasted goats, a barrel of cakes and nine mince pies will do me until dinnertime."

Kaliko bowed and hurried away to the royal kitchen, forgetting Tiktok, who was wandering around in the outer cavern. Suddenly the Nome King looked up and saw the Clockwork Man standing before him, and at the sight the monarch's eyes grew big and round and he fell a-trembling in every limb.

"Away, grim Shadow!" he cried. "You're not here, you know; you're only a hash of cogwheels and springs, lying at the bottom of the black pit. Vanish, thou Vision of the demolished Tiktok, and leave me in peace—for I have bitterly repented!"

"Then beg my pardon," said Tiktok in a gruff voice, for Kaliko had forgotten to oil the speech works.

But the sound of a voice coming from what he thought a mere vision was too much for the Nome King's shaken nerves. He gave a yell of fear and rushed from the room. Tiktok followed, so the King bolted through the corridors on a swift run and bumped against Kaliko, who was returning with a tray of things to eat. The sound of the breaking dishes, as they struck the floor, added to the King's terror and he yelled again and dashed into a great cavern where a thousand Nomes were at work hammering metal.

"Look out! Here comes a phantom clockwork man!" screamed the terrified

monarch, and every Nome dropped his tools and made a rush from the cavern, knocking over their King in their mad flight and recklessly trampling upon his prostrate fat body. So, when Tiktok came into the cavern, there was only the Nome King left, and he was rolling upon the rocky floor and howling for mercy, with his eyes fast shut so that he could not see what he was sure was a dreadful phantom that was coming straight toward him.

"It oc-curs to me," said Tiktok calmly, "that your Maj-es-ty is act-ing like a ba-by. I am not a phan-tom. A phan-tom is un-real, while I am the real thing."

The King rolled over, sat up and opened his eyes.

"Didn't I smash you to pieces?" he asked in trembling tones.

"Yes," said Tiktok.

"Then you are nothing but a junk-heap, and this form in which you now appear can-not be real."

"It is, though," declared Tiktok. "Kal-i-ko picked up my piec-es and put me to-geth-er a-gain. I'm as good as new, and perhaps bet-ter."

"That is true, your Majesty," added Kaliko, who now made his appearance, "and I hope you will forgive me for mend-ing Tiktok. He was quite broken up, after you smashed him, and I found it almost as hard a job to match his pieces as to pick turnips from gooseberry bushes.

But I did it," he added proudly.

"You are forgiven," announced the Nome King, rising to his feet and drawing a long breath. "I will raise your wages one specto a year, and Tiktok shall return to the Land of Oz loaded with jewels for the Princess Ozma."

"That is all right," said Tiktok. "But what I want to know is, why did you hit me with your mace?"

"Because I was angry," admitted the King. "When I am angry I always do something that I am sorry for afterward. So I have firmly resolved never to get angry again; unless—unless—"

"Unless what, your Majesty?" inquired Kaliko.

"Unless something annoys me," said the Nome King. And then he went to his treasure-chamber to get the jewels for Princess Ozma of Oz.

OZMA AND THE LITTLE WIZARD

NCE upon a time there lived in the beautiful Emerald City, which lies in the center of the fairy Land of Oz, a lovely girl called Princess Ozma, who was ruler of all that country. And among those who served this girlish Ruler and lived in a cozy suite of rooms in her splendid palace, was a little, withered old man known as the Wizard of Oz.

This little Wizard could do a good many queer things in magic; but he was a kind man, with merry, twinkling eyes and a sweet smile; so, instead of fearing him because of his magic, everybody loved him.

Now, Ozma was very anxious that all her people who inhabited the pleasant Land of Oz should be happy and contented, and therefore she decided one morning to make a journey to all parts of the country, that she might discover if anything was amiss, or anyone discontented, or if there was any wrong that ought to be righted. She asked the little Wizard to accompany her and he was glad to go.

"Shall I take my bag of magic tools with me?" he asked.

"Of course," said Ozma. "We may need a lot of magic before we return, for we are going into strange corners of the land, where we may meet with unknown creatures and dangerous adventures."

So the Wizard took his bag of magic tools and the two left the Emerald City and wandered over the country for many days, at last reaching a place far up in the mountains which neither of them had ever visited before. Stopping one morning at a cottage, built beside the rocky path which led into a pretty valley beyond, Ozma asked a man:

"Are you happy? Have you any complaint to make of your lot?"

And the man replied:

"We are happy except for three mischievous Imps that live in yonder valley and often come here to annoy us. If your Highness would only drive away those Imps, I and my family would be very happy and very grateful to you."

"Who are these bad Imps?" inquired the girl Ruler.

"One is named Olite, and one Udent and one Ertinent, and they have no respect for anyone or anything. If strangers pass through the valley, the Imps jeer at them and make horrid faces and call names, and often they push travelers out of the path or throw stones at them. Whenever Imp Olite or Imp Udent or Imp Ertinent comes here to bother us, I and my family run into the house and lock all the doors and windows, and we dare not venture out again until the Imps have gone away."

Princess Ozma was grieved to hear this report and the little Wizard shook his head gravely and said the naughty Imps deserved to be punished. They told the good man they would see what could be done to protect him and at once entered the valley to seek the dwelling place of the three mischievous creatures.

Before long they came upon three caves, hollowed from the rocks, and in front of each cave squatted a queer little dwarf. Ozma and the Wizard paused to examine them and found them well-shaped, strong and lively. They had big round ears, flat

noses and wide grinning mouths, and their jet-black hair came to points on top of their heads, much resembling horns. Their clothing fitted snugly to their bodies and limbs and the Imps were so small in size that at first Ozma did not consider them at all dangerous. But one of them suddenly reached out a hand and caught the dress of the Princess, jerking it so sharply that she nearly fell down, and a moment later another Imp pushed the little Wizard so hard that he bumped against Ozma and both unexpectedly sat down upon the ground.

At this the Imps laughed boisterously and began running around in a circle and kicking dust upon the Royal Princess, who cried in a sharp voice: "Wizard, do your duty!"

The Wizard promptly obeyed. Without rising from the ground he opened his bag, got the tools he required and muttered a magic spell.

Instantly the three Imps became three bushes—of a thorny, stubby kind—with their roots in the ground. As the bushes were at first motionless, perhaps through surprise at their sudden transformation, the Wizard and the Princess found time to rise from the ground and brush the dust off their pretty clothes. Then Ozma turned to the bushes and said:

"The unhappy lot you now endure, my poor Imps, is due entirely to your naughty actions. You can no longer annoy harmless travelers and you must remain ugly bushes, covered with sharp thorns, until you repent of your bad ways and promise to be good Imps.”

“They can’t help being good now, your Highness,” said the Wizard, who was much pleased with his work, “and the safest plan will be to allow them always to remain bushes.”

But something must have been wrong with the Wizard’s magic, or the creatures had magic of their own, for no sooner were the words spoken than the bushes began to move. At first they only waved their branches at the girl and little man, but pretty soon they began to slide over the ground, their roots dragging through the

earth, and one pushed itself against the Wizard and pricked him so sharply with its thorns that he cried out: "Ouch!" and started to run away.

Ozma followed, for the other bushes were trying to stick their thorns into her legs and one actually got so near her that it tore a great rent in her beautiful dress. The girl Princess could run, however, and she followed the fleeing Wizard until he tumbled head first over a log and rolled upon the ground. Then she sprang behind a tree and shouted: "Quick! Transform them into something else."

The Wizard heard, but he was much confused by his fall. Grabbing from his bag the first magical tool he could find he transformed the bushes into three white pigs. That astonished the Imps. In the shape of pigs—fat, roly-poly and cute—they scampered off a little distance and sat down to think about their new condition.

Ozma drew a long breath and coming from behind the tree she said:

"That is much better, Wiz, for such pigs as these must be quite harmless. No one need now fear the mischievous Imps."

"I intended to transform them into mice," replied the Wizard, "but in my excitement I worked the wrong magic. However, unless the horrid creatures behave themselves hereafter, they are liable to be killed and eaten. They would make good chops, sausages or roasts."

But the Imps were now angry and had no intention of behaving. As Ozma and the little Wizard turned to resume their journey, the three pigs rushed forward, dashed between their legs, and tripped them up, so that both lost their balance and toppled over, clinging to one another. As the Wizard tried to get up he was tripped again and fell across the back of the third pig, which carried him on a run far down the valley until it dumped the little man in the river. Ozma had been sprawled upon the ground but found she was not hurt, so she picked herself up and ran to the assistance of the Wizard, reaching him just as he was crawling out of the river, gasping for breath and dripping with water. The girl could not help laughing at his woeful appearance. But he had no sooner wiped the wet from his eyes than one of the impish pigs tripped him again and sent him into the river for a second bath. The pigs tried to trip Ozma, too, but she ran around a stump and so managed to keep out of their way. So the Wizard scrambled out of the water again and picked up a sharp stick to defend himself. Then he mumbled a magic mutter which instantly dried his clothes, after which he hurried to assist Ozma. The pigs were afraid of the sharp stick and kept away from it.

"This won't do," said the Princess. "We have accomplished nothing, for the pig Imps would annoy travelers as much as the

real Imps. Transform them into something else, Wiz."

The Wizard took time to think. Then he transformed the white pigs into three blue doves.

"Doves," said he, "are the most harmless things in the world."

But scarcely had he spoken when the doves flew at them and tried to peck out their eyes. When they endeavored to shield their eyes with their hands, two of the doves bit the Wizard's fingers and another caught the pretty pink ear of the Princess in its bill and gave it such a cruel tweak that she cried out in pain and threw her skirt over her head.

"These birds are worse than pigs, Wizard," she called to her companion. "Nothing is harmless that is animated by impudent anger or impertinent mischief. You must transform the Imps into something that is not alive."

The Wizard was pretty busy, just then, driving off the birds, but he managed to open his bag of magic and find a charm which instantly transformed the doves into three buttons. As they fell to the ground he picked them up and smiled with satisfaction. The tin button was Imp Olite, the brass button was Imp Udent and the lead button was Imp Ertinent. These buttons the Wizard placed in a little box which he put in his jacket pocket.

"Now," said he, "the Imps cannot annoy

travelers, for we shall carry them back with us to the Emerald City."

"But we dare not use the buttons," said Ozma, smiling once more now that the danger was over.

"Why not?" asked the Wizard. "I intend to sew them upon my coat and watch them carefully. The spirits of the Imps are still in the buttons, and after a time they will repent and be sorry for their naughtiness. Then they will decide to be very good in the future. When they feel that way, the tin button will turn to silver and the brass to gold, while the lead button will become aluminum. I shall then restore them to their proper forms, changing their names to pretty names instead of the ugly ones they

used to bear. Thereafter the three Imps will become good citizens of the Land of Oz and I think you will find they will prove faithful subjects of our beloved Princess Ozma."

"Ah, that is magic well worthwhile," exclaimed Ozma, well pleased. "There is no doubt, my friend, but that you are a very clever Wizard."

JACK PUMPKINHEAD AND THE SAWHORSE

N a room of the Royal Palace of the Emerald City of Oz hangs a Magic Picture, in which are shown all the important scenes that transpire in those fairy dominions. The scenes shift constantly, and by watching them, Ozma, the girl Ruler, is able to discover events taking place in any part of her kingdom.

One day she saw in her Magic Picture
that a little girl and a little boy had wandered together into a great, gloomy forest
at the far west of Oz and had become hope-
lessly lost. Their friends were seeking them
in the wrong direction and unless Ozma
came to their rescue the little ones would
never be found in time to save them from
starving.

So the Princess sent a message to Jack
Pumpkinhead and asked him to come to
the palace. This personage, one of the
queerest of the queer inhabitants of Oz,
was an old friend and companion of Ozma.
His form was made of rough sticks fitted
together and dressed in ordinary clothes.
His head was a pumpkin with a face carved

upon it, and was set on top a sharp stake which formed his neck.

Jack was active, good-natured and a general favorite; but his pumpkin head was likely to spoil with age, so in order to secure a good supply of heads he grew a big field of pumpkins and lived in the middle of it, his house being a huge pumpkin hollowed out. Whenever he needed a new head he picked a pumpkin, carved a face on it and stuck it upon the stake of his neck, throwing away the old head as of no further use.

The day Ozma sent for him Jack was in prime condition and was glad to be of service in rescuing the lost children. Ozma made him a map, showing just where the forest was and how to get to it and the

paths he must take to reach the little ones. Then she said:

"You'd better ride the Sawhorse, for he is swift and intelligent and will help you accomplish your task."

"All right," answered Jack, and went to the royal stable to tell the Sawhorse to be ready for the trip.

This remarkable animal was not unlike Jack Pumpkinhead in form, although so different in shape. Its body was a log, with four sticks stuck into it for legs. A branch at one end of the log served as a tail, while in the other end was chopped a gash that formed a mouth. Above this were two small knots that did nicely for eyes. The Sawhorse was the favorite steed of Ozma and to prevent its wooden legs from wearing out she had them shod with plates of gold.

Jack said "Good morning" to the Sawhorse and placed upon the creature's back a saddle of purple leather, studded with jewels.

"Where now?" asked the horse, blinking its knot eyes at Jack.

"We're going to rescue two babes in the wood," was the reply. Then he climbed into the saddle and the wooden animal pranced out of the stable, through the streets of the Emerald City and out upon the highway leading to the western forest where the children were lost.

Small though he was, the Sawhorse was

swift and untiring. By nightfall they were in the far west and quite close to the forest they sought. They passed the night standing quietly by the roadside. They needed no food, for their wooden bodies never became hungry; nor did they sleep, because they never tired. At daybreak they continued their journey and soon reached the forest.

Jack now examined the map Ozma had given him and found the right path to take, which the Sawhorse obediently followed. Underneath the trees all was silent and gloomy and Jack beguiled the way by whistling gayly as the Sawhorse trotted along.

The paths branched so many times and in so many different ways that the Pumpkin-

head was often obliged to consult Ozma's map, and finally the Sawhorse became suspicious.

"Are you sure you are right?" it asked.

"Of course," answered Jack. "Even a Pumpkinhead whose brains are seeds can follow so clear a map as this. Every path is plainly marked, and here is a cross where the children are."

Finally they reached a place, in the very heart of the forest, where they came upon the lost boy and girl. But they found the two children bound fast to the trunk of a big tree, at the foot of which they were sitting.

When the rescuers arrived, the little girl was sobbing bitterly and the boy was trying to comfort her, though he was probably frightened as much as she.

"Cheer up, my dears," said Jack, getting out of the saddle. "I have come to take you back to your parents. But why are you bound to that tree?"

"Because," cried a small, sharp voice, "they are thieves and robbers. That's why!"

"Dear me!" said Jack, looking around to see who had spoken. The voice seemed to come from above.

A big grey squirrel was sitting upon a low branch of the tree. Upon the squirrel's head was a circle of gold, with a diamond set in the center of it. He was running up and down the limbs and chattering excitedly.

"These children," continued the squirrel,

angrily, "robbed our storehouse of all the nuts we had saved up for winter. Therefore, being King of all the Squirrels in this forest, I ordered them arrested and put in prison, as you now see them. They had no right to steal our provisions and we are going to punish them."

"We were hungry," said the boy, pleadingly, "and we found a hollow tree full of nuts, and ate them to keep alive. We didn't want to starve when there was food right in front of us."

"Quite right," remarked Jack, nodding his pumpkin head. "I don't blame you one bit, under the circumstances. Not a bit."

Then he began to untie the ropes that bound the children to the tree.

"Stop that!" cried the King Squirrel, chattering and whisking about. "You mustn't release our prisoners. You have no right to."

But Jack paid no attention to the protest. His wooden fingers were awkward and it took him some time to untie the ropes. When at last he succeeded, the tree was full of squirrels, called together by their King, and they were furious at losing their prisoners. From the tree they began to hurl nuts at the Pumpkinhead, who laughed at them as he helped the two children to their feet.

Now, at the top of this tree was a big dead limb, and so many squirrels gathered upon it that suddenly it broke away and fell to

the ground. Poor Jack was standing direct-
ly under it and when the limb struck him it
smashed his pumpkin head into a pulpy
mass and sent Jack's wooden form tum-
bling, to stop with a bump against a tree a
dozen feet away.

He sat up, a moment afterward, but
when he felt for his head it was gone. He
could not see; neither could he speak. It was
perhaps the greatest misfortune that could
have happened to Jack Pumpkinhead, and
the squirrels were delighted. They danced
around in the tree in great glee as they saw
Jack's plight.

The boy and girl were indeed free, but
their protector was ruined. The Sawhorse
was there, however, and in his way he was

wise. He had seen the accident and knew that the smashed pumpkin would never again serve Jack as a head. So he said to the children, who were frightened at this accident to their new found friend:

"Pick up the Pumpkinhead's body and set it on my saddle. Then mount behind it and hold on. We must get out of this forest as soon as we can, or the squirrels may capture you again. I must guess at the right path, for Jack's map is no longer of any use to him since that limb destroyed his head."

The two children lifted Jack's body, which was not at all heavy, and placed it upon the saddle. Then they climbed up behind it and the Sawhorse immediately turned and trot-

ted back along the path he had come, bearing all three with ease. However, when the path began to branch into many paths, all following different directions, the wooden animal became puzzled and soon was wandering aimlessly about, without any hope of finding the right way. Toward evening they came upon a fine fruit tree, which furnished the children a supper; and at night the little ones lay upon a bed of leaves while the Sawhorse stood watch, with the limp, headless form of poor Jack Pumpkinhead lying helpless across the saddle.

Now, Ozma had seen in her Magic Picture all that had happened in the forest, so she sent the little Wizard, mounted upon the Cowardly Lion, to save the unfortunates. The Lion knew the forest well and when he reached it he bounded straight through the tangled paths to where the Sawhorse was wandering, with Jack and the two children on his back.

The Wizard was grieved at the sight of the headless Jack, but believed he could save him. He first led the Sawhorse out of the forest and restored the boy and girl to the arms of their anxious friends, and then he sent the Lion back to Ozma to tell her what had happened.

The Wizard now mounted the Sawhorse and supported Jack's form on the long ride to the pumpkin field. When they arrived at Jack's house the Wizard selected a fine pumpkin—not too ripe—and very neatly

carved a face on it. Then he stuck the pumpkin solidly on Jack's neck and asked him:

"Well, old friend, how do you feel?"

"Fine!" replied Jack, and shook the hand of the little Wizard gratefully. "You have really saved my life, for without your assistance I could not have found my way home to get a new head. But I'm all right, now, and I shall be very careful not to get this beautiful head smashed." And he shook the Wizard's hand again.

"Are the brains in the new head any better than the old ones?" inquired the Sawhorse, who had watched Jack's restoration.

"Why, these seeds are quite tender,"

replied the Wizard, "so they will give our friend tender thoughts. But, to speak truly, my dear Sawhorse, Jack Pumpkinhead, with all his good qualities, will never be noted for his wisdom."

THE SCARECROW AND
THE TIN WOODMAN

 HERE lived in the Land of Oz two queerly made men who were the best of friends. They were so much happier when together that they were seldom apart; yet they liked to separate, once in a while, that they might enjoy the pleasure of meeting again.

One was a Scarecrow. That means he was a suit of blue Munchkin clothes, stuffed with straw, on top of which was fastened a round cloth head, filled with bran to hold it in shape. On the head were painted two eyes, two ears, a nose and a mouth. The Scarecrow had never been much of a success in scaring crows, but he prided himself on being a superior man, because he could feel no pain, was never tired and did not have to eat or drink. His brains were sharp, for the Wizard of Oz had put pins and needles in the Scarecrow's brains.

The other man was made all of tin, his arms and legs and head being cleverly jointed so that he could move them freely. He was known as the Tin Woodman, having at one time been a woodchopper, and everyone loved him because the Wizard had given him an excellent heart of red plush.

The Tin Woodman lived in a magnificent tin castle, built on his country estate in the Winkie Land, not far from the Emerald City of Oz. It had pretty tin furniture and was surrounded by lovely gardens in which were many tin trees and beds of tin flowers. The palace of the Scarecrow was not far distant, on the banks of a river, and this palace was in the shape of an immense ear of corn.

One morning the Tin Woodman went to visit his friend the Scarecrow, and as they had nothing better to do they decided to take a boat ride on the river. So they got into the Scarecrow's boat, which was formed from a big corncob, hollowed out and pointed at both ends and decorated around the edges with brilliant jewels. The sail was of purple silk and glittered gayly in the sunshine.

There was a good breeze that day, so the boat glided swiftly over the water. By and by they came to a smaller river that flowed from out a deep forest, and the Tin Wood-man proposed they sail up this stream, as it would be cool and shady beneath the trees of the forest. So the Scarecrow, who was steering, turned the boat up the stream and the friends continued talking together of old times and the wonderful adventures they had met with while traveling with Dorothy, the little Kansas girl. They be-came so much interested in this talk that they forgot to notice that the boat was now sailing through the forest, or that the stream was growing more narrow and crooked.

Suddenly the Scarecrow glanced up and saw a big rock just ahead of them.

"Look out!" he cried; but the warning came too late.

The Tin Woodman sprang to his feet just as the boat bumped into the rock, and the jar made him lose his balance. He toppled and fell overboard and being made of tin he sank to the bottom of the water in an instant and lay there at full length, face up.

Immediately the Scarecrow threw out the anchor, so as to hold the boat in that place, and then he leaned over the side

and through the clear water looked at his friend sorrowfully.

"Dear me!" he exclaimed; "what a misfortune!"

"It is, indeed," replied the Tin Woodman, speaking in muffled tones because so much water covered him. "I cannot drown, of course, but I must lie here until you find a way to get me out. Meantime, the water is soaking into all my joints and I shall become badly rusted before I am rescued."

"Very true," agreed the Scarecrow; "but be patient, my friend, and I'll dive down and get you. My straw will not rust, and is easily replaced, if damaged, so I'm not afraid of the water."

The Scarecrow now took off his hat and

made a dive from the boat into the water; but he was so light in weight that he barely dented the surface of the stream, nor could he reach the Tin Woodman with his outstretched straw arms. So he floated to the boat and climbed into it, saying the while:

"Do not despair, my friend. We have an extra anchor aboard, and I will tie it around my waist, to make me sink, and dive again."

"Don't do that!" called the tin man. "That would anchor you also to the bottom, where I am, and we'd both be helpless."

"True enough," sighed the Scarecrow, wiping his wet face with a handkerchief; and then he gave a cry of astonishment, for he found he had wiped off one painted eye

and now had but one eye to see with.

"How dreadful!" said the poor Scarecrow. "That eye must have been painted in water-color, instead of oil. I must be careful not to wipe off the other eye, for then I could not see to help you at all."

A shriek of elfish laughter greeted this speech and looking up the Scarecrow found the trees full of black crows, who seemed much amused by the straw man's one-eyed countenance. He knew the crows well, however, and they had usually been friendly to him because he had never deceived them into thinking he was a meat man—the sort of man they really feared.

"Don't laugh," said he; "you may lose an eye yourselves some day."

"We couldn't look as funny as you, if we did," replied one old crow, the king of them. "But what has gone wrong with you?"

"The Tin Woodman, my dear friend and companion, has fallen overboard and is now on the bottom of the river," said the Scarecrow. "I'm trying to get him out again, but I fear I shall not succeed."

"Why, it's easy enough," declared the old crow. "Tie a string to him and all of my crows will fly down, take hold of the string, and pull him up out of the water. There are hundreds of us here, so our united strength could lift much more than that."

"But I can't tie a string to him," replied the Scarecrow. "My straw is so light that I am unable to dive through the water.

I've tried it, and knocked one eye out."

"Can't you fish for him?"

"Ah, that is a good idea," said the Scarecrow. "I'll make the attempt."

He found a fishline in the boat, with a stout hook at the end of it. No bait was needed, so the Scarecrow dropped the hook into the water till it touched the Woodman.

"Hook it into a joint," advised the crow, who was now perched upon a branch that stuck far out and bent down over the water.

The Scarecrow tried to do this, but having only one eye he could not see the joints very clearly.

"Hurry up, please," begged the Tin Woodman; "you've no idea how damp it is down here."

"Can't you help?" asked the crow.

"How?" inquired the tin man.

"Catch the line and hook it around your neck."

The Tin Woodman made the attempt and after several trials wound the line around his neck and hooked it securely.

"Good!" cried the King Crow, a mischievous old fellow. "Now, then, we'll all grab the line and pull you out."

At once the air was filled with black crows, each of whom seized the cord with beak or talons. The Scarecrow watched them with much interest and forgot that he had tied the other end of the line around his own waist, so he would not lose it while fishing for his friend.

"All together for the good caws!" shrieked the King Crow, and with a great flapping of wings the birds rose into the air.

The Scarecrow clapped his stuffed hands in glee as he saw his friend drawn from the water into the air; but the next moment the straw man was himself in the air, his stuffed legs kicking wildly; for the crows had flown straight up through the trees. On one end of the line dangled the Tin Woodman, hung by the neck, and on the other dangled the Scarecrow, hung by the waist and clinging fast to the spare anchor of the boat, which he had seized hoping to save himself.

"Hi, there—be careful!" shouted the Scarecrow to the crows. "Don't take us

so high. Land us on the river bank."

But the crows were bent on mischief. They thought it a good joke to bother the two, now that they held them captive.

"Here's where the crows scare the Scarecrow!" chuckled the naughty King Crow, and at his command the birds flew over the forest to where a tall dead tree stood higher than all the other trees. At the very top was a crotch, formed by two dead limbs, and into the crotch the crows dropped the center of the line. Then, letting go their hold, they flew away, chattering with laughter, and left the two friends suspended high in the air—one on each side of the tree.

Now the Tin Woodman was much heavier than the Scarecrow, but the reason they balanced so nicely was because the straw man still clung fast to the iron anchor. There they hung, not ten feet apart, yet unable to reach the bare tree-trunk.

"For goodness sake don't drop that anchor," said the Tin Woodman anxiously.

"Why not?" inquired the Scarecrow.

"If you did I'd tumble to the ground, where my tin would be badly dented by the fall. Also you would shoot into the air and alight somewhere among the tree-tops."

"Then," said the Scarecrow, earnestly, "I shall hold fast to the anchor."

For a time they both dangled in silence, the breeze swaying them gently to and fro. Finally the tin man said: "Here is an emergency, friend, where only brains can help us. We must think of some way to escape."

"I'll do the thinking," replied the Scarecrow. "My brains are the sharpest."

He thought so long that the tin man grew tired and tried to change his position, but found his joints had already rusted so badly that he could not move them. And his oil-can was back in the boat.

"Do you suppose your brains are rusted, friend Scarecrow?" he asked in a weak voice, for his jaws would scarcely move.

"No, indeed. Ah, here's an idea at last!"

And with this the Scarecrow clapped his hands to his head, forgetting the anchor, which tumbled to the ground. The result was astonishing; for, just as the tin man had said, the light Scarecrow flew into the air, sailed over the top of the tree and land-ed in a bramble-bush, while the tin man fell plump to the ground, and landing on a bed of dry leaves was not dented at all. The Tin Woodman's joints were so rusted, however, that he was unable to move, while the thorns held the Scarecrow a fast prisoner.

While they were in this sad plight the sound of hoofs was heard and along the for-est path rode the little Wizard of Oz, seated on a wooden Sawhorse. He smiled when he saw the one-eyed head of the Scarecrow sticking out of the bramble-bush, but he helped the poor straw man out of his prison.

"Thank you, dear Wiz," said the grateful Scarecrow. "Now we must get the oil-can and rescue the Tin Woodman."

Together they ran to the river bank, but the boat was floating in midstream and the Wizard was obliged to mumble some magic words to draw it to the bank, so the Scarecrow could get the oil-can. Then back they flew to the tin man, and while the Scarecrow carefully oiled each joint the little Wizard moved the joints gently back and forth until they worked freely. After an hour of this labor the Tin Woodman was again on his feet, and although still a little stiff he managed to walk to the boat.

The Wizard and the Sawhorse also got aboard the corncob craft and together they returned to the Scarecrow's palace. But the Tin Woodman was very careful not to stand up in the boat again.

AFTERWORD

No more stories from Oz? That's what L. Frank Baum had told his readers in 1910 at the end of his *The Emerald City of Oz*. After ten years and six novels, Baum wanted to write about other fantastic lands and amazing characters. So at the conclusion of *Emerald City,* having moved Dorothy, Aunt Em, and Uncle Henry to Oz for good, he had Glinda magically turn all of Oz invisible, cutting it off from the rest of the world forever.

Was this truly the last story about Oz?

Of course not! Baum was no more successful at ending the Oz series than Sir Arthur Conan Doyle had been at killing off Sherlock Holmes nearly twenty years earlier. Readers did not care what the creator of Oz wanted. Having journeyed to the most fabulous fairyland ever, they were determined to visit again and again, and they deluged Baum with requests for more stories about Oz.

Baum, however, was not so easily swayed. In 1911, he published *The Sea Fairies,* the first title in what he hoped would be a new series of stories for all the young readers who loved his Oz books. Featuring a young girl named Trot and her peg-legged old sailor friend, Cap'n Bill, the story described their adventures under the waves when they are befriended by mermaids. Though filled with the same imagination and humor as his Oz books and beautifully illustrated by Oz artist John R. Neill, Baum's readers were not satisfied and the book's sales were disappointing.

For the following year, Baum wrote a new adventure, *Sky Island,* about Trot and Cap'n Bill. Keenly aware that his Oz fans missed their favorite characters and desiring to draw them to his struggling new series, Baum brought Button Bright and Polychrome (two popular characters from his fifth Oz book, *The Road to Oz*) into the story. But Baum's readers were still not satisfied. They wanted Oz.

So in 1913, Baum finally acquiesced to the demands of his "loving tyrants" and returned to Oz. Not only did he write the seventh full-length Oz book, *The Patchwork Girl of Oz*, but he issued six shorter Oz stories for younger readers.

These six short stories were dubbed the "Little Wizard Stories" and were reissued the following year, bound together in one volume under the title *Little Wizard Stories of Oz*. Brightly illustrated with numerous full-color pictures by John R. Neill, these smaller tales allowed Baum to explore the fascinating personalities of the delightful characters he had created in the previous six Oz books, without the burden of a lengthy, sustained plot.

Many of the most wonderful attributes of Baum's best characters are allowed to fully shine here in these stories. In "The Cowardly Lion and the Hungry Tiger," we get to see once and for all what humbugs these giant felines are. And though the Scarecrow may have sharp brains and the Tin Woodman may be bright (especially when well polished), Baum makes it very clear in their story that it is their friendship and love for each other that makes these two gentlemen so appealing.

Humor is also at a high pitch in these fast-paced gems. In addition to the delightful turnabout of the boasting Lion and Tiger and the slapstick antics of the Scarecrow and Tin Woodman, there is the hilarious sight of the ill-tempered Nome King running in terror from what he believes to be the ghost of Tiktok—a mechanical man who was never alive in the first place. And of course the very names of those three nasty imps—Olite, Udent, and Ertinent—that the Wizard and Ozma have to contend with in their tale are enough to bring a smile to the face of even the most stoic individual.

As in all good collections of fairy tales—

and that is what the *Little Wizard Stories* are—there are moments of suspense and danger. The Sawhorse's flight through the forest to escape the angry squirrels, with a headless Jack Pumpkinhead and the two rescued children, is guaranteed to send young hearts racing, and when Dorothy breaks all those dishes at Crinklink's house, a shiver of fear for her safety is keenly felt by all.

But, unlike the darker fairy tales of Grimm and Perrault, in Baum's Oz fairy tales the danger quickly passes and everything is put to rights. True to his introduction in *The Wonderful Wizard of Oz,* Baum has avoided any truly "disagreeable incidents" or "horrible and blood-curdling" moments in these stories.

Of course, part of the fun of any Oz book is the pictures. And no one has ever equaled John R. Neill in capturing the magic, humor, and beauty of Oz. In forty-five full-color drawings—including six double-page spreads—Neill has breathed life into Baum's extraordinary creations while adding marvelously imaginative touches all his own.

So here you have in your hands six of Baum's finest little stories, all in one volume. Baum's young readers had triumphed. The creator of Oz had returned to his fabulous fairyland and taken us with him. But how was this possible? After all, wasn't Oz still invisible and cut off from the

rest of the world? How did these stories get
to "The Royal Historian of Oz" from Oz?
The answer will be found in the next Oz
book, *The Patchwork Girl of Oz.*

—*Peter Glassman*

OZ TITLES IN THE
BOOKS OF WONDER
SERIES

THE WONDERFUL WIZARD OF OZ
by L. Frank Baum

with 24 full-color plates and over 130 two-color illustrations
by W.W. Denslow

THE MARVELOUS LAND OF OZ
by L. Frank Baum

with 16 full-color plates and over 125 black-and-white illustrations
by John R. Neill

OZMA OF OZ
by L. Frank Baum

with 42 full-color and 21 two-color illustrations
by John R. Neill

DOROTHY AND THE WIZARD IN OZ
by L. Frank Baum

with 16 full-color plates and 50 black-and-white illustrations
by John R. Neill

THE ROAD TO OZ
by L. Frank Baum
with 126 black-and-white illustrations
by John R. Neill

THE EMERALD CITY OF OZ
by L. Frank Baum
with 15 full-color plates and 90 black-and-white illustrations
by John R. Neill

DOROTHY OF OZ
by Roger S. Baum
with full-color frontispiece and 50 black-and-white illustrations
by Elizabeth Miles

If you enjoy the Oz books and want to know more about Oz, you may be interested in The Royal Club of Oz. Devoted to America's favorite fairyland, it is a club for everyone who loves the Oz books. For free information, please send a first-class stamp to:

THE ROYAL CLUB OF OZ
P.O. Box 714
New York, New York 10011

or call toll free: (800) 835-4315

BOOKS OF WONDER
CLASSICS

---

by LEWIS CARROLL
Alice's Adventures in Wonderland
illustrated by John Tenniel
Through the Looking-glass and What Alice Found There
illustrated by John Tenniel

by CHARLES DICKENS
Oliver Twist illustrated by Don Freeman

by SIR ARTHUR CONAN DOYLE
The Adventures of Sherlock Holmes illustrated by Barry Moser
The White Company illustrated by N.C. Wyeth

by WASHINGTON IRVING
The Legend of Sleepy Hollow illustrated by Arthur Rackham
Rip Van Winkle illustrated by N.C. Wyeth

by ANDREW LANG
The Rainbow Fairy Book illustrated by Michael Hague

by GEORGE MacDONALD
At the Back of the North Wind
illustrated by Jessie Willcox Smith
The Princess and the Goblin
illustrated by Jessie Willcox Smith

by E. NESBIT
The Enchanted Castle illustrated by Paul O. Zelinsky

by EDGAR ALLAN POE
Tales of Edgar Allan Poe illustrated by Barry Moser

by MARK TWAIN
The Adventures of Tom Sawyer illustrated by Barry Moser
A Connecticut Yankee in King Arthur's Court
illustrated by Trina Schart Hyman

by JULES VERNE
Around the World in Eighty Days illustrated by Barry Moser

by OSCAR WILDE
The Happy Prince and Other Stories
illustrated by Charles Robinson